For Chloë and Beth Williams
C.C.
For M & D at 33
and M & D at LGB
P.W.

HERBERT BINNS
& THE FLYING TRICYCLE

CAROLINE CASTLE & PETER WEEVERS

DIAL BOOKS FOR YOUNG READERS
New York

Herbert Binns was very small, even for a mouse, but he didn't care. Because Herbert Binns was a most clever mouse. He could do double somersaults, read backwards, and sing and play the accordion; but what he liked best was inventing. Herbert Binns was a brilliant inventor.

M ost animals loved Herbert Binns, but there
were three—McTabbity, an old rabbit; Zip,
a greedy young rat; and Measly, a mean old weasel—
who didn't like him at all. They were jealous that
one animal could be more talented than all three
of them. And whenever they saw Herbert, they
would taunt him with a rhyme:

Herbert Binns is so horribly small
That no one cares for him at all.

But Herbert simply made up a rhyme on the spur of the moment and replied:

Herbert Binns may be smaller than you,
But look what this tiny mouse can do!
He goes head over heels, he can play and sing,
And best of all he'll invent anything!

The three animals could never think of anything to say in return and at Herbert's words they would storm off, stamping their feet and feeling furious that someone so small and unimportant looking could be so smart.

One afternoon, Zip, Measly, and McTabbity were sitting in their secret den, talking about their favorite subject.

"That Herbert Binns," said McTabbity, "is too small for his boots."

"Have you heard his latest scheme?" said Zip.

"No! What?" said the others eagerly. The affairs of Herbert Binns were always of great interest to them.

"Well," said Zip, lowering his voice to a whisper, "he says he's invented a flying tricycle, and he's going to test it next Thursday afternoon."

"A flying tricycle!" roared McTabbity in a furious rabbity voice. "Who does he think he is!"

Of course, the gang had never thought of inventing a flying tricycle themselves—in fact, they rarely thought about anything other than Herbert Binns. Without Herbert to get angry about, their lives would have been quite dull.

So they gathered round to think how Herbert could be fixed for good.

The next day Herbert Binns was in his workshop, poring over his plans for the flying tricycle. As he worked he sang:

> If birds and bees and tops of trees
> Are things you specially like,
> If you like a breeze around your knees
> You'll need Binns's flying trike.

"Mustn't forget my special starting pin," he muttered to himself. "Very important for a smooth takeoff."

What he didn't see, however, was a whiskery face at the window. It was McTabbity, and he was writing down every word that Herbert Binns said.

Zip and Measly were sitting at Vole's waterside restaurant when McTabbity came rushing up. "I have here all we need to put that mouse in his place," he cried, and he read aloud from his piece of paper.

Ha!" said Zip, chugging down a whole glass of barley juice in one gulp. "Special pin, eh? Let's steal it—then won't he look silly when his wonderful tricycle doesn't take off?"
And he laughed a ratty laugh.

The three animals turned to look at the poster that was stuck on an old willow in the middle of the restaurant:

HERBERT BINNS
MOUSE AND INVENTOR
WILL BE DEMONSTRATING HIS
SPECTACULAR FLYING TRICYCLE
NEXT THURSDAY AFTERNOON
DOWN BY THE RIVERSIDE
ALL WELCOME

"That's what he thinks!" sneered McTabbity.

That night, as Herbert Binns slept peacefully,
the three animals crept up to his house.
   Zip and Measly kept watch, while McTabbity
silently squeezed himself through the workshop
window.

He looked in Herbert's desk drawers; he looked under the carpet; he looked inside Herbert's box of treasures on the shelf and found nothing. He was just about to give up when he spotted Herbert's jacket hanging up behind the door. He reached inside the pocket and his paw touched something cold and hard. The special pin!

That very second an owl hooted and a cloud crept over the moon. McTabbity began to get the jitters. Quickly he grabbed the special pin and scrambled out through the tiny window.

Back in the den with Zip and Measly, McTabbity danced in excitement. "Thinks he's clever, that Binns," he chortled. "But some animals are more clever—like me!" And he took the special pin from his pocket.

Zip and Measly admired McTabbity's good work. At last Herbert Binns was going to get his comeuppance.

The three animals were so excited that they could hardly wait for Thursday to arrive. Whenever they saw some animals reading the poster, they called out with glee:

Be sure to be there, be sure to be there,
When the minuscule mouse takes to the air.

Thursday afternoon arrived at last. Down by the riverside, the crowd had gathered, and a banner was tied between two trees which said:

THE ANIMALS OF FIELD EDGE WISH
HERBERT BINNS
THE BEST OF LUCK
ON HIS MAIDEN
VOYAGE

"He'll need it," sneered McTabbity.

"We couldn't have picked a better plan," said Zip. "The whole town of Field Edge is here to watch him make a fool of himself. He won't dare show his little whiskery face in public again."

At that moment, the most wonderful machine appeared on the hill. It was a green tricycle with two enormous wings that flapped beautifully— and riding it was Herbert Binns.

Zip, Measly, and McTabbity couldn't stop
laughing as Herbert reached into his waistcoat
pocket.

He felt around for a minute, and he pulled out
the special pin.

"What . . ." said Zip.

"How . . ." gasped Measly.

"It can't be!" cried McTabbity.

Herbert looked at the three animals in turn, then he said in his most sensible voice:

You rabbity McTabbity,
You're daffier than a hare.
You didn't think I'd risk your tricks!
You see—I've got a spare!

And with that he inserted the special pin and the flying tricycle glided into the air as gracefully as a bird.

McTabbity, Zip, and Measly raged and gnashed their teeth.

"We'll get him *next* time," said Measly.

"Never fear," agreed Zip.

"That stupid—" screamed McTabbity.

But we'll never know what McTabbity said because his voice was drowned by the cheers of the crowd as Herbert Binns, the wings of his tricycle flapping beautifully, disappeared over the tops of the trees.

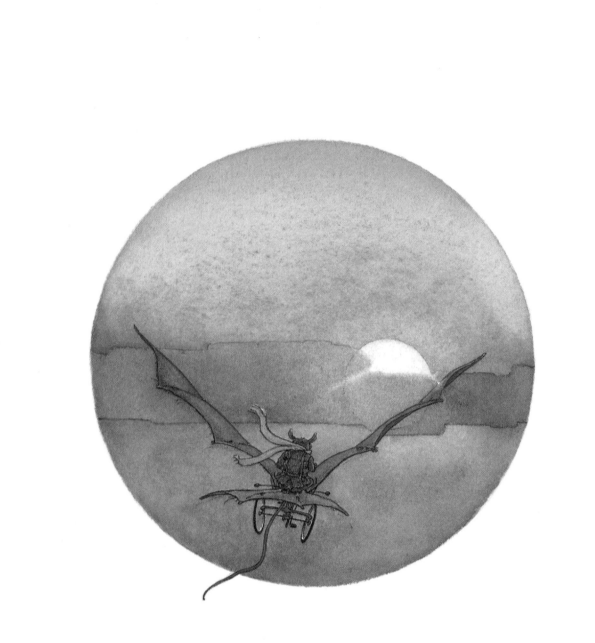

833661

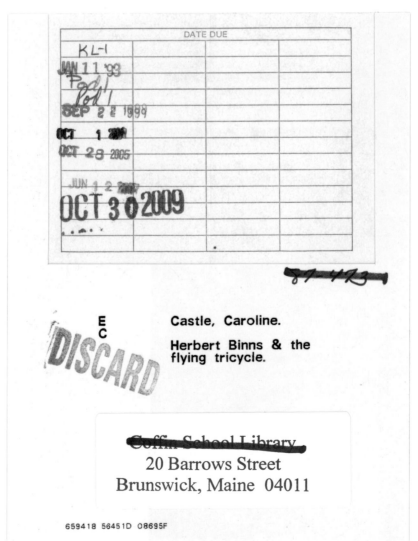